Jack and Jill

Distributed by The Child's World®
1980 Lookout Drive • Mankato, MN 56003-1705
800-599-READ • www.childsworld.com

Acknowledgments
The Child's World®: Mary Berendes, Publishing Director
The Design Lab: Kathleen Petelinsek, Design and Page Production

Library of Congress Cataloging-in-Publication Data
Woodruff, Liza.
  Jack and Jill / by Liza Woodruff.
      p. cm.
  Summary: A retelling of the classic nursery rhyme, with end notes on the
identity and origins of Mother Goose.
  ISBN 978-1-60253-536-7 (library bound : alk. paper)
  1. Nursery rhymes. 2. Children's poetry. [1. Nursery rhymes.] I. Mother
Goose. II. Title.
  PZ8.3.W8919Jac 2010
  398.8—dc22   2010014157

Printed in the United States of America in Mankato, Minnesota.
July 2010
F11538

ILLUSTRATED BY LIZA WOODRUFF

Jack and Jill went up
the hill,

4

to fetch a pail of water.

Jack fell down

and broke his crown,

and Jill came
tumbling after.

ABOUT MOTHER GOOSE

We all remember the Mother Goose nursery rhymes we learned as children. But who was Mother Goose, anyway? Did she even exist? The answer is . . . we don't know! Many different tales surround this famous name.

Some people think she might be based on Goose-footed Bertha, a kindly old woman in French legend who told stories to children. The inspiration for this legend might have been Queen Bertha of France, who died in 783 and whose son Charlemagne ruled much of Europe. Queen Bertha was called Big-footed Bertha or Queen Goosefoot because one foot was larger than the other.

The name "Mother Goose" first appeared in Charles Perrault's *Les Contes de ma Mère l'Oye* ("Tales of My Mother Goose"), published in France in 1697. This was a collection of fairy tales including "Cinderella" and "Sleeping Beauty"—but these were stories, not poems. The first published Mother Goose nursery rhymes appeared in England in 1781, as *Mother Goose's Melody; or Sonnets for the Cradle*. But some of the verses themselves are hundreds of years old, passed along by word of mouth.

Although we don't really know the origins of Mother Goose or her nursery rhymes, we *do* know that these timeless verses are beloved by children everywhere!

Liza Woodruff has been illustrating children's books for thirteen years. She lives in Vermont in an old farmhouse with her husband, two children, a cat, a dog, two guinea pigs, and three chickens. Liza is constantly inspired by her children and pets, and the farm country where they all live.